Hooting, Tooting Dinosaurs

Adapted by Andrea Posner-Sanchez
from the episode "Call of the Wild Corythosaurus"

Based on the television series created by Craig Bartlett

Illustrated by Paul Conrad

A GOLDEN BOOK • NEW YORK

TM & © 2011 The Jim Henson Company. JIM HENSON'S mark & logo, DINOSAUR TRAIN mark & logo, characters and elements are trademarks of The Jim Henson Company. All Rights Reserved. The PBS KIDS logo is a registered mark of Public Broadcasting Service (PBS)® 2011. Published in the United States by Golden Books, an imprint of Random House Children's Books, a division of Random House, Inc., 1745 Broadway, New York, NY 10019, and in Canada by Random House of Canada Limited, Toronto. Golden Books, A Golden Book, A Little Golden Book, the G colophon, and the distinctive gold spine are registered trademarks of Random House, Inc.
www.randomhouse.com/kids
pbskids.org/dinosaurtrain
ISBN: 978-0-375-86153-6
Printed in the United States of America
10 9 8 7 6 5 4 3

One day, Buddy, Shiny, Tiny, and Don were playing outside the nest when their dad walked up to them.

"I've found the perfect birthday present for Mom," said Mr. Pteranodon. "Tickets to a music concert at Corythosaurus Canyon!"

Mr. Pteranodon explained that the Corythosaurus is a dinosaur that makes its own special musical noises.

"I bet they make music with their feet and tails," suggested Shiny.

Everyone went to tell Mom about her birthday gift.
"That's wonderful!" exclaimed Mrs. Pteranodon.

The next morning, the whole family got on the Dinosaur Train. Mr. Conductor collected their tickets. "I see you're heading to a concert," he said. "Be sure to ask a Corythosaurus about its crest."

"What is a crest?" asked Buddy.

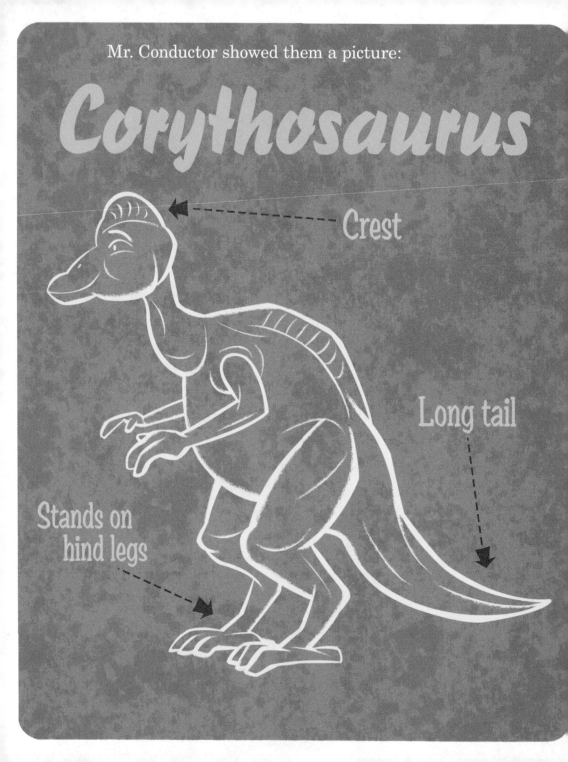

When the Pteranodon family got off the train, they saw some Corythosaurus heading toward them.

"Hi, we're Mr. and Mrs. Corythosaurus," said the mother dinosaur, "and this is our daughter, Cory."

"Are you here for the concert?" Cory asked.
"We sure are!" responded Mr. Pteranodon.
"Um, Cory? Can we see your crest?" Buddy asked shyly.

Cory bowed her head to show off her crest to her new friends. "Pretty cool, huh?"

Then while Shiny stayed with the grown-ups, Cory took Buddy, Tiny, and Don on a tour of the canyon. As they walked around, the siblings asked more questions about Cory's crest.

"Do you use it to breathe underwater?"

"Is it a princess crown?"

"Does it have something to do with your Corythosaurus music?"

"Yes, Tiny!" Cory said. "I breathe air in and it travels all around and through my crest. Then it comes out and sounds like . . ."

All of a sudden, they heard hoots coming from a distance. *HOOT!* Cory hooted back.

"Corythosaurus communicate by hooting," Cory explained. "My mom just hooted to tell me that it's almost time for the concert."

"Before we go, let's play hide-and-hoot," Cory suggested. "I'll hide and you have to guess where I am."

Buddy, Tiny, and Don closed their eyes. Cory hid behind a tree. *HOOT!* The kids opened their eyes and ran to the tree. But Cory had already moved to a different spot.

"Hmm. It sounded like she was here!" said Buddy.

HOOT! They ran to a rock.
Cory wasn't there, either.
Everyone laughed as they
ran around and around,
trying to find Cory.

HOOT!

"That's my mom again," Cory said. "Time to go to the concert."

"Hooray!" cheered Tiny. "I can't wait to hear you play music with your crest, Cory!"

Buddy, Tiny, and Don joined the rest of their
family in front of the stage.

"Gosh, I'm so excited!" said Mrs. Pteranodon.

"Happy birthday, hon!" Mr. Pteranodon told her.

"Welcome to our Corythosaurus concert!" Cory's mom said to the audience. "We are so glad you all are here!"

Then the concert began. All the hooting and tooting sounded great together. And everyone loved Cory's dad's deep hoots.

"Now it's time for Cory's solo!" Cory's mom announced from the stage.

Little Cory looked nervous. But she made terrific high-pitched hoots all by herself. The Pteranodon family cheered.

When the concert ended, Buddy got an idea. He whispered to his brother and sisters. Then he said, "Mom, we have another present for you."

Buddy, Shiny, and Don hooted as Tiny sang:
"Happy birthday, Mom! Here's your birthday song.
It's really short; it's not too long.
We've got a crest; it's like a flute.
Listen to it hoot and toot!"

HOOT

TOOT

HOOT

TOOT